CORNELL DYER AND THE FLU

An *Adventures of Cornell Dyer*
supernatural mystery

Denise M. Baran-Unland

In collaboration with
Timothy M. Baran

Illustrated by Sue Midlock

This book is lovingly dedicated to the reader, whoever you might be.

"Ghost of the Future, I fear you more than any specter I have seen. But as I know your purpose is to do me good, and as I hope to live to be another man from what I was, I am prepared to bear you company, and do it with a thankful heart. - **Charles Dickens**

TABLE OF CONTENTS

Prologue

Epilogue

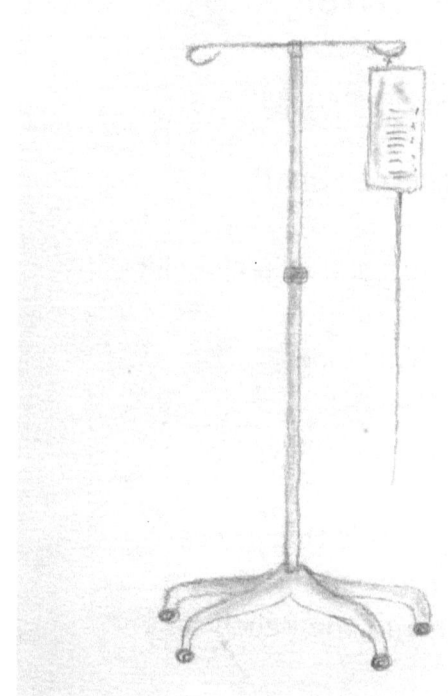

PROLOGUE

IV pole

Glaring lights. Gleaming metal.

Am avenue of white cabinets.

Clear plastic tubes.

Beep. Beep. Beep.

Lots and lots of slow-dripping tubes.

"Sir, can you hear me?"

An impassioned face.

Crinkling. Crackling. The smell of alcohol.

And quarternary ammonium disinfectant.

"Sir?"

EEEEEEEEEEEEEEEEEEEEEEEEEEEEE
EEEEEEEEEEEEEEEEEEEEEEEEEEEEEEEEE
EEEEEEE!!!

"I need help here!"

A muzzle. Hissing.

Giant marshmallows rushing in circles.

"What happened?"

"Clear!

Bounce! Bounce! Bounce!

"We're losing him!"

CHAPTER ONE: SNACKING TO DEATH

Cornell Dyer opened another bag of potato chips, mixed another orange drink, and settled back to watch the action.

What a fuss!

Doctors and nurses, all dressed in white and looking like marshmallows with arms and legs, huddled around him, pressing, poking, prodding.

He felt a pinch, and another pinch, and another, but none of the pinches hurt.

He opened his mouth and popped some chips, even though he wore a clear mask and two paddles kept jumping on his chest.

He gulped another drink.

High up in the corner of the room was

a television, turned to a news station, volume low, too low for Cornell to hear the voice of the weatherman.

Cornell yawned and reached for another bag of chips, wishing they'd hurry up. He had a supernatural mystery to solve.

The marshmallows had their volume turned down, too. They moved their mouths, but no sound came out.

The entire room was bustling, bright, and deathly quiet.

Cornell reached for his last orange drink, but it was empty. He was out of potato chips, too. Time to find a vending machine!

He swung his legs over the side of the narrow bed, set his bare feet on the floor, stood, and felt a tug. He was caught on one of the cords!

Except this cord was different from the rest.

The cords plugged into the wall were black. The tubes attached to his body were clear and oozed clear liquid.

This special cord was a golden cord, and it was attached to both versions of him.

For although Cornell was standing on

the floor, knee deep in crumpled potato chip bags and empty orange drink bottles, he was also still lying in the hospital bed, with the golden cord connecting them.

And this was no ordinary cord.

Not that golden cords were ordinary.

But this golden cord was especially extraordinary.

It twinkled and sparked bright golden lights with silent crackles.

The numbers on the machines dropped.

The lines on the machines straightened.

Only the marshmallows moved faster.

They had cords, too, just like his. As they rushed, their cords wove among the other cords, but the cords did not hamper their movements as they hampered Cornell's.

Instead, their cords grew longer and shorter with each bustling step, just like a toy yo-yo.

"Eureka!" Cornell cried without sound.

He knew how to unsnag himself.

Cornell gently pulled on his end of the cord. And just like unraveling thread on a spool, more of the snapping golden line glided out of him.

Now to find that vending machine.

He passed through the marshmallows as if they were ghosts. The tile floor on Cornell's feet did not feel cold.

Oh, no!

Cornell had left his wallet in the motor home, and he could not remember where he parked.

In fact, he could not remember driving to the hospital.

What could he remember? Why was he here?

Cornell paused, the only two people in the entire room not moving. He thought hard, and the gears in his head cranked.

He saw his bedroom in the motor home. The room was dark except for the green glow of the phone dial, and the luminous dream fairies flitting through the rooms.

"Madam!" Cornell had exploded into the phone. 'Do you understand what time it is?"

"Yes! But it's the only time they talk!" the voice on the other end wailed. "Please

come right away and make them go away!"

"That's impossible!"

"Impossible? Aren't you the world-famous supernatural super sleuth, the great Professor Cornell Dyer?"

"Madam, that is true, but..."

"And aren't you skilled with amulets, fortune-telling (with and without cards), ghost-hunting, horoscopes, numerology, palm-reading, potions, séances, spells, and vampire-slaying?"

"Madam, that is true, but..."

"Then why won't you come to my house and get rid of the voices?"

"Because it's three o'clock in the morning! I never go to work without a good night's rest and a really good breakfast!"

"The voices will be gone by then!"

"Good night!"

But had he gone back to sleep? Had he eaten breakfast? Cornell could not remember.

Probably not, the reason Cornell's stomach grumbled with extreme hunger. But without his wallet, he could not buy potato chips and an orange drink from the vending machine.

And then Cornell saw someone who gave him hope.

Across the room, an old man with tufts of white hair and a white mustache was writing at an old maple desk.

The man wore a green and red plaid bathrobe. A bit of white T-shirt peeked through the top of the robe.

A little silver desk lamp illuminated the sheet of paper, providing the only light in the dark corner of that room.

Next to the lamp stood a miniature chipped ceramic Christmas tree. Cornell did not decorate his motor home for Christmas, nor did he buy Christmas trees, even though Christmas was approaching.

Cornell had no time for such nonsense, not with so many supernatural mysteries that needing solving.

But maybe the man had a quarter for the vending machine. The man looked gentle and kind, the sort of man who would happily help a starving man with his last quarter, especially at Christmas.

Cornell decided it wouldn't hurt to ask.

He carefully stepped over all the empty paper chip bags and bottles of empty orange drinks. Even though he was already lying inside a hospital, it wouldn't do to slip and break his back.

"Excuse me, sir," Cornell began.

The man kept writing. "The name is Charlie. Charlie Charleston."

"Mr. Charleston, would you…"

The man held his hand up. "Please. Call me 'Charlie.'"

"Excuse me, Charlie. Would you happen to have…"

The man set the pen aside and studied Cornell. "My wife's name was Mabel."

Cornell sighed in deep frustration and starvation. But before Cornell turned away, he noticed something.

He noticed Charlie's robe was faded and frayed. He noticed Charlie's eyes were tired and sad.

Charlie probably didn't have any money to lend and felt embarrassed.

Maybe Cornell could ask a nurse in the hall. Maybe he could borrow enough to buy a bag of chips and a bottle of orange drink for Charlie, too.

"Look at me," Charlie said in a stern voice that made Cornell jump.

"What?"

"I said look at me. What do you see?"

"I see an old, white-haired man in a bathrobe sitting at a desk who won't let me ask him for a quarter for the vending machine."

"No, no! You're focusing on the outside. What do you see?"

Cornell bent down and stared at the man's blue eyes. They were bright now and a little moist, and his face wore an eager smile.

"I still see an old, white-haired man in a bathrobe sitting at a desk who won't let me ask him for a quart..."

The smile faded, a little.

"Professor, I'm a man in love. I'm in love with my wife Mable." Charlie gestured to the paper. "And I'm writing..."

"A love letter! You're writing a love letter to Mable."

Maybe now Charlie would lend him that quarter.

Charlie's smile softened, and his eyes crinkled in a pleasing way.

"I am. You see, Professor, Mable had to leave me for a little while. But I'm writing her a letter on this Christmas Eve to tell her I'll be joining her soon. Do you see my tree?

Charlie gestured to the old chipped ceramic Christmas tree.

"Mabel made this tree for me with her very own hands over seventy years ago, for our very first Christmas, when we had no money to buy presents for each other."

"It's very nice. Charlie. But would you have a…"

"She put her heart and soul into this gift, Professor. I've treasured it all these years. Let's walk."

It's about time, Cornell thought.

Charlie clicked off the light, stood up, tightened the sash to his robe, slid his feet into a pair of scuffs, and picked up his golden cord, which curved this way and that over most of the floor on that part of the room.

"To the vending machine?"

"Sure, Professor."

Cornell was so happy, he scarcely gave a backward glance at the silent bustling around his immobile self, still lying on the bed at the other end of the room.

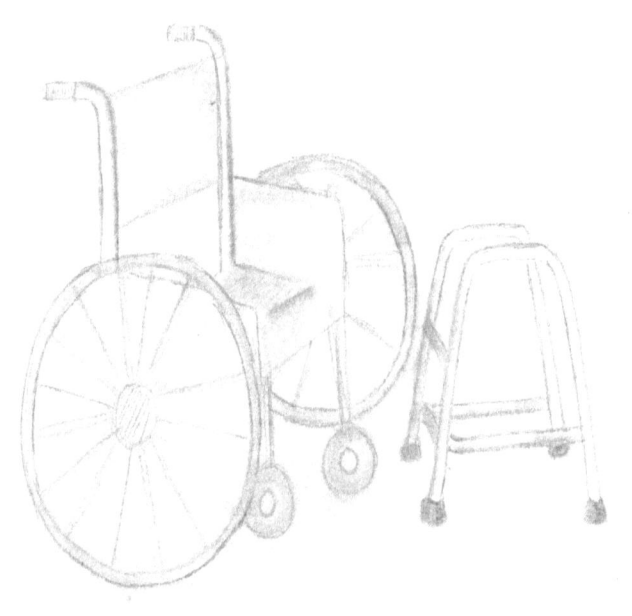

CHAPTER TWO: WALKERS AND WHEELCHAIRS

This was not Cornell's first time in a hospital.

But it was Cornell's first time in a hospital like this one.

Doctors gave instructions to nurses or wrote in charts, just like in regular hospitals.

Nurses checked charts, answered phones, and talked to the patients' families at the desk, just like in regular hospitals.

Some nurses pushed patients in wheelchairs to their rooms. Others pushed patients on beds with wheels down the hall.

They did these activities like nurses in regular hospitals did them.

But all these events reminded Cornell of the television set in the room where his other self still lay.

The television set with the volume turned down.

All the doctors, nurses, and visitors moved their mouths, but no sound came out.

Cornell heard no rumble of wheels from the chairs or beds.

He hard no voices on the loudspeaker or beeping of machines.

But he did hear crackling.

The crackling came from the golden cords of the health care team and their patients.

But although every cord was golden, not every cord was the same.

Some cords looked thicker than others and sparked with vibrant golden lights.

The thinner cords had weak sizzles

and dull blinking lights, as if those efforts zapped all the cord's energy.

A few tattered cords had lost their sheen and had split into sepia threads, ready to snap.

Most of the hospital staff had strong golden cords, except for the charge nurse. Her cord, although thick, had a little tarnish.

"She has cancer," Charlie said. "But she doesn't know it yet."

They rounded the corner, and Cornell nearly tripped. He glanced back and saw why. His cord was much shorter than Charlies and hindered his steps.

"Just give it a little tug," Charlie said. "But be gentle. You don't want to sever it. It's not your time yet."

Cornell grasped his cord in one hand. It felt solid, secure, not likely to tear. Nevertheless, he gave it a gentle tug as Charlie instructed him and proceeded down the hall.

They passed several elderly people pushing walkers. Some had vibrant cords, some had frail.

One tiny wrinkled woman with a brave

smile dragged the most delicate cord of them all. But she took halting brave steps and did not trip on the vulnerable thread.

"Can she get a new one?" Cornell asked.

Charlie shook his head. "I'm afraid not, Professor. We only get one cord. Look."

He stopped in front of a hotel room and gestured to a bed where a young man was peacefully sleeping.

The man's cord lay in two dried shriveled pieces on the floor. As Cornell watched, the man wafted away from himself with a blissful grin and floated out of the window.

Cornell turned to Charlie. "What kind of hospital is this?"

"It's just a regular hospital, Professor."

Charlie is lying, Cornell thought. Why would such a nice man lie?

As they resumed their walk, Cornell thought back to the time he collapsed from copper poisoning from the necklace of forgetfulness.

He wound up in the hospital that time, too. But Cornell could hear every doctor. He could hear every nurse. He could hear every person who visited him.

He also could hear the telephone when it rang, and he could hear the cry for his help on the other end of the line.

The telephone line, which Cornell could see.

Not golden cords, which Cornell did not see at that hospital.

"This is not a regular hospital, Charlie."

"Sure it is." Charlie gestured around him. "It has doctors, nurses, patients, loved ones. Some people get well and go home. And some people get well in other ways and go to their eternal home."

"What about the golden cords? I've never seen cords like this in a hospital."

"The golden cords have nothing to do with the hospital, Professor. Here, look."

Charlie stopped in front of another room, and Cornell peered into another room. He saw a woman frantically trying to climb into her body. Her cord, too, lay broken and useless on the floor.

Cornell thought of his other body lying in the emergency department and grabbed Charlie's arm.

"Let's go back. What if I can't..."

"Return to your body?" Charlie picked up Cornell's cord and held it high. "It's nice and strong. You'll get in."

Charlie let Cornell's cord go, and it wafted to the floor.

Cornell noticed Charlie's cord had shrunk and turned bronze.

"Charlie, why did your cord...?"

"Professor, let's walk."

They proceeded on their silent way, with a starving Cornell wondering when they would reach the vending machine.

That's when Cornell noticed the others. These people, as shriveled as old pear cores, floated a couple inches over the floors with sightless eyes, their stiff brown cords trailing them.

If this was a hospital like any other hospital, why was Cornell noticing cords for the first time? Why hadn't he seen them in other hospitals, too?

Maybe Charlie was special, and he was helping Cornell be special, too.

But Cornell was a supernatural super sleuth. All cords, golden or not, should be always be visible to him.

"Charlie, could you always see the cords?"

"No, Professor. Ordinary men like men don't get to see the cords".

"You don't seem ordinary to me."

Charlie stopped and lightly touched Cornell's shoulder. He smiled softly. "'Charlie Charleston.' What kind of name is that? What kind of parents give a kid a name like that, huh?"

Cornell shrugged and braced himself for a boring story.

"You know, Professor, what amazes me is the way we're all connected. If I'd realized it years ago, why I would have…"

Abruptly, Charlie jerked to a halt. He tugged very lightly on his cord, which was splitting at random sections.

"I'm afraid this is where we must part. But if you go this way," Charlie's eyes drooped as pointed down the hall. He also swayed, slightly.

Charlie's voice also sounded weak as he added, "If you go this way, you'll soon find yourself in the emergency department and back inside your body.

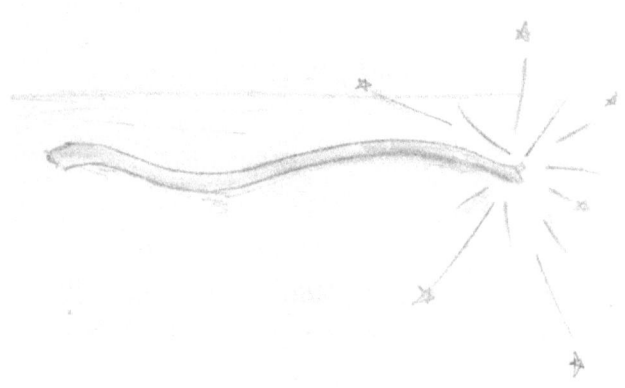

CHAPTER THREE: ON A THIN LINE

Cornell trudged the way Charlie indicated, annoyed the old man had picked this moment to go back to his room for a nap.

At least, Cornell assumed Charlie wanted a nap. Charlies had looked exhausted.

Hoping to pass a vending machine, and a kind nurse who would buy potato chips and an orange drink for him, Cornell marveled at the interconnectedness of all the golden cords. Each cord tangled with the others and yet remained free.

Halfway to his destination, Cornell caught a glint out of his eye.

It wasn't an ordinary glint, like glass in the sunlight or his pocketknife under the desk lamp.

It was like the glint in a werewolf's eye before it attacked.

I was right, Cornell thought. This is no ordinary hospital. Because most hospitals don't have werewolves.

Even though Cornell lay in a hospital bed somewhere far away from himself, he was still a supernatural super sleuth.

And supernatural super sleuths do not miss an opportunity for solving supernatural mysteries.

Besides, he was famished, and he needed to find a vending machine. Maybe the glint came from a quarter on the floor.

He turned left to a dim hallway to discover the source of the mysterious glint and, hopefully, a vending machine.

Down, down, down the hallway that grew darker with every step, except for glint, a determined Cornell walked, glancing left and right for spare coins.

On and on Cornell strode, miles, it seemed to him, miles and miles for days and days.

Cornell was walking along a passageway that had no apparent end.

The cord freely flowed from his body and did not snag, a cord as endless as the hall.

The glint did not grow brighter. But it grew bigger until Cornell reached the end and could go no further.

One large section of the wall was glass, which gave a view of exposed beams, elevator cables, and, way, way, way at the very bottom, a laboratory of sorts.

Cornell pressed his nose against the glass and peered down at the various testing tubes, some with clear fluid, some with red, and some with mist rising from them.

Hospital beds jammed together among the tubes. People lay on their beds, eyes wide in fear, their gold cords snapping with life.

Hordes of white kittens merrily romped throughout the room or hung from the ceiling lights, watching the fun.

Their cords, black and wet with decay, tangled with the gold cords, not hampering their movements in the least.

A short, stooped man with wire glasses and auburn hair and mutton chops was scurrying around beds and cats, cutting

strong golden cords with shiny silver sharp
scissors and then soaking the cords into the
bloody vials before reattaching cords,
joining each person to a cat.

A pipe peeked from the man's white
lab coat pocket, a beautiful pipe of polished
dark wood and gleaming gold trim.

Splotches of reds as well as
florescent greens smeared the man's white
lab coat.

The reattached cords glowed green,
like cat eyes at night.

Or a werewolf before it attacked.

The new cords caused human limbs to
twitch and mist to drift from mouths and
nostrils.

Cornell heard a hum, like the sound of
a vacuum cleaner, after one plugged its
extension cord into the wall and flipped the
switch.

Strange, Cornell thought.

The cats continued playing and
prancing as if they were frolicking in a
spring meadow instead of a subterranean
laboratory.

His own cord crackled gold in the void.

And his empty stomach grumbled with

impatience.

But at least Cornell now knew the source of the glint.

The glowing green cords.

CHAPTER FOUR: OPPOSITES ATTRACT

"We're losing him!"

Cornell stood in the stairwell and stared at the note, scratching his head.

In his very own handwriting, he read the words, "Go this way."

He had also drawn an arrow, pointing to the door.

Cornell shuffled up the stairs, opened the door, and found himself standing in the middle of an empty cafeteria lit by a single, dangling bulb, which cast dancing shadows on all the walls.

The bulb exploded.

Mist rose from the floor.

His ears buzzed as he read the note.

Go this way.

"We're losing him!"

Cornell jiggled the handle. It was unlocked. He stepped into the exam room and saw the note, waiting for him, right where he left it.

Even the ghosts hadn't disturbed it.

Go this way.

The gleam on his golden cord had dulled to bronze and grown brittle in spots. Instead of sparking, it merely winked and not often or consistently.

The buzz grew louder.

A tiny patter of feet ran past him.
A child giggled.

"We heard you saved him," one nurse said. "How'd you know he wasn't faking?

"We didn't. That's why we ordered pizza first. He wasn't going to fool us again."

Go this way.

The walk darkened, but only at the corner of his vision, even though no one had turned on the overhead lights.

The globed lights made up for it. They now lined each hall and room, blazing with brilliant white light.

Coughing in his ear.
Chittering all around him.
An echoing pound of footsteps.

Go this way.

The gold threads squeaked as they unraveled, and the cord resisted Cornell's movements, as Charlie's cord had resisted his.

Shadows with arms outstretched passed through him and glided down the hall.

Where was the emergency room???

Cornell glanced at the fragile threads of his gold cord.

An empty wheelchair rolled away.

The droning of a million electrical cords.

Cornell covered his ears to block the sound and gasped for real this time, frozen in horror as he gazed down the other side of the hall.

HAPTER FIVE: DARKNESS IS DANGEROUS

Nothing.

That's what Cornell saw.

Nothing.

In a hospital that should be busy caring for the sick, Cornell saw nothing.

No doctors and nurses. No patients. No cords of gold, no cords of any kind.

Even the ghosts had vanished.

Cornell was the only being in this very large, empty hospital, and he could not even find his way back to himself.

At once, the droning stopped.

Cornell lowered his ears; his eyes frantically seeking the note, the note he left the last time he passed this way.

A little light *clink* made him nearly jump out of his skin.

His heart hammered; he breathed hard.

The globe next to him had begun to tinkle, the light little tinkle of a fairy wind chime on a mild summer day.

Clinkety-clinkety-clinkety-clinkety...

One by one, the other globes, picked up the call, an orchestra of singing lights, harmonizing a call Cornell could not resist.

CHUNG!

The light farthest away had blown into splintering glass, and the others followed.

CHUNG-----CHUNG---CHUNG--CHUNGCHUNGCHUNG...

Cornell screamed and buried his face in his sleeve.

He felt a light touch, a familiar touch.

Cornell felt a touch he never expected to feel ever again.

And he heard a friendly voice, the friendliest voice he had ever heard, a voice he had never expected to hear ever again.

It's the fever, Cornell told himself. The last time he heard that voice, Cornell had a fever.

That was a fact, as true as any fact recorded by Donald B. Pemberton at the Cape Crag Historical Society.

Cornell turned, and there he was.

"Every time we meet, you're always in trouble," Jack said with a friendly wink. "Maybe this time, I can repay the favor."

CHAPTER SIX: A TRIP TO THE BEACH

What a heavenly day!

Sunny rays streaked a sky of clearest blue, the perfect background for the perfect cottony clouds drifting across it.

At Cornell's left, a smooth path, bordered by fragrant gardens of colorful flowers every hue the mind can imagine, and a few more it cannot, wound away to a paradise he couldn't wait to explore.

The gentlest of waves rippled across the blue-green lake and sloshed against the boat.

The air smelled clean, fresh, and twittered with the sounds of happy birds.

Cornell felt happy, calm, and alive as he reclined on his beach chair under a wide umbrella, near a little tin pail and plastic shovel and a sandcastle with turrets and moats, reveling in just being.

Reclining on a beach chair, and also under an umbrella, was Jack of all Trades.

Jack's skin was pink and smooth.

His hair was wet and blond.

His eye was sound and open.

His fingers were whole and unharmed.

His leg was straight and strong.

His sandy blond hair fluttered in the light breeze. He emitted light and vibrancy.

And Jack was smiling his usual friendly smile.

Jack was near him and, yet, he was out of reach.

"I'm so happy to see you, Jack," Cornell said.

Jack laughed, a bubbly laugh that made Cornell want to laugh, too.

"I'm happy to see you, too, friend," Jack said in a voice that sounded farther away than he appeared.

"But I didn't think I'd see you for a long, long time yet," Jack continued. "Are you sure you're supposed to be here?"

Cornell sighed happily. "Who cares? It's perfect here. Wait. What's that noise?"

"What noise?" Jack asked, still smiling.

Cornell cocked his head. The noise grew louder. "It's a whine. No, wait. It's a siren."

"Don't worry about it, Professor," Jack said. "You'll hear it every now and then, but it doesn't last long. I don't mind hearing it anymore. Probably because I've lived in these parts a very long time."

The siren grew louder. Cornell's inner alarm grew bigger.

"What parts, Jack?"

But Jack just smiled.

Cornell reached out to grab Jack's arm and missed. Jack was still sitting on the beach chair beside Cornell, but now he appeared very far away.

"You have to decide, Professor," Jack said. Even though he was smiling, his voice sounded grave. "You're running out of time."

Cornell looked across the water. He recognized the lake. He remembered the invisible barrier that kept him from this beach.

He decided.

Cornell jumped up and started running

to his room.

Right down the noisy hall of doctors and nurses caring for their sick patients.

Cornell needed to get to his room, not to the other side of the lake.

That was for later. That was for someday.

Alive, he thought to himself.

Alive, alive. I've got to stay alive.

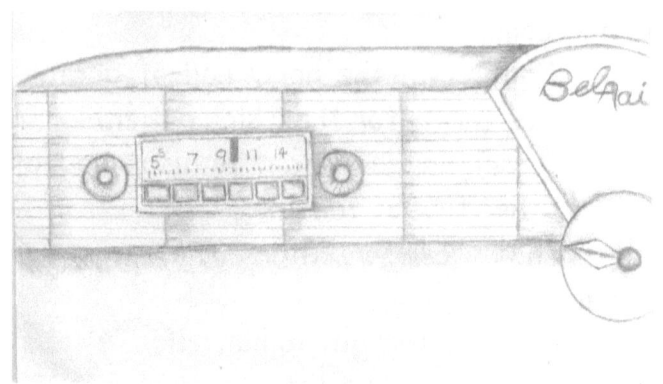

CHAPTER SEVEN: SUDDEN SHOCKS

HONK! HONK-HONK HONK!

Cornell pulled down the visor against the sun's glare and reached for the window handle.

He'd already rolled down the window as far as it would go, less than halfway, but he yanked it anyway, hoping he could force it loose and tease a breeze from the sultry air.

"Professor, we're stuck for the duration," Charlie grinned at him from his place behind the steering wheel. "So relax."

Cornell grunted and glowered as he shielded his eyes. So many cars!

Sport cars and family cars; pick-up trucks and dump drunks, all merged in one confusing backed-up highway mess of a road construction time trap.

"Dreadful apparition," Cornell grumbled, "Why do you trouble me?"

Charlie grinned. "Marley's ghost. I read 'A Christmas Carol,' too. Didn't think I was that smart, did you?"

Before Cornell could retort, Charlie gestured at the traffic. "Look at them. They travel without rest, without peace. Just one long eternal stretch."

Cornell rolled his eyes and slumped against the hot cushion. His hospital gown stuck to his sweaty back; the seatbelt dug into his neck.

He started to unbuckle it until he noticed the police officer sitting on the motorcycle anywhere.

Cornell stayed buckled. And uncomfortable.

And hungry and thirsty.

Despite the smell of garbage, Cornell didn't see any food or drink, except for the cold coffee in the cupholder. Maybe Charlie had snacks in the trunk. Eternity was a long time.

Charlie turned to Cornell and smiled.

"But you, Professor, can escape their fate."

Cornell snorted and switched on the radio.

"Charlie, are you sending me three Christmas ghosts?"

Maybe he could find a Wagnerian opera to lift his mood. He moved the sticky knob around and around, but the only music emitting from the crackling speakers was rollicking Christmas music played very badly on accordions.

"Three beings will visit you, Professor, but they are not the ghosts of Christmas Past, Christmas Present, and Christmas Future."

Charlie still draped one hand on the wheel, as if he expected the jam to ease anytime soon.

About five minutes later, the cars began to inch along the road.

"Where are the ghosts?" Cornell asked impatiently.

"I told you, Professor," Charlie said with a grin. He looked cool and happy, not hot and irritated. "These are visitors. Not ghosts."

"When are they appearing?"

"I'm taking you to the first one."

"And where is that?"

"Next exit. Twenty miles ahead."

At that moment, all vehicles slammed to a stop.

Again.

For the hundredth time that day.

The sun had nearly set, and twilight had nearly arrived by the time Charlie exited the long highway and pulled into a gas station.

Finally! Snacks!

For Cornell never did find that vending machine, and he was famished to the point of collapse.

"Thanks, Charlie," a very familiar voice called out. "You're right on time, as always. I'll take over from here."

CHAPTER EIGHT: GRANDPA MO

"Grandpa Mo!" Cornell cried. "Grandpa Mo, how did you get here?"

This was not the young version of Grandpa Mo, or Mike Olsen, with his brown hair and freckles, a young man not too short and not too tall, that Cornell had met on a previous adventure.

This was Mike Olsen near the end of his life, as Cornell knew him when Cornell

44

was a little boy.

This Mike Olson had white hair, a paunch in the middle of his bent frame, and he stood on thin, shaky legs.

"Let me see your pocket watch," Grandpa Mo said with a quaver in his old voice.

Cornell pulled out his old gold watch, the one Grandpa Mo had given Cornell before Grandpa had died.

Grandpa Mo said, "Do you remember what I told you?"

Cornell rolled his eyes. He was tired of playing games. But maybe if he played, Grandpa Mo would take him to the candy store, like he did when Cornell was young.

"You told me to be good with time," Cornell said. "And I have. I take good care of the watch and keep it wound, but I never over-wind it."

Grandpa Mo looked sad. "You are good with the watch, but you are not good with time. Being good with time means using each second this pocket watch ticks to bless another."

"But Grandpa Mo! I am a supernatural sleuth. I travel everywhere in my motor home solving supernatural mysteries for people! I use time very well!"

"You use time for yourself," Grandpa Mo pointed to the distance. "Does this look familiar?"

Cornell saw himself, about eight, consulting a crystal ball for the answers to his math test.

Cornell saw himself, about twelve, reading a biography on Harry Houdini while Grandma Maddie hobbled out to the trash with the kitchen garbage, even though she had asked Cornell twelve times to do it.

Cornell saw himself, about seventeen, standing up his prom date because he bought a new magic trick he wanted to practice.

Cornell saw himself, a young man, charging lots of money for magic potions that contained only cheap, very weak magic.

Cornell saw Lucille DuBois washing mountains of his laundry that Cornell should have washed himself.

"I know you've helped a lot of people, Cornell," Grandpa Mo said. "But you've missed out on the most important part of life.

"It's true," a thick syrupy voice piped

up.

Oh, no, Cornell thought. It couldn't be.

He whirled around.

There stood Larry the Llama, munching a wad of grass off his hoof.

CHAPTER NINE: LARRY THE LLAMA

"You!" Cornell cried. "What are you doing here?

"Well, I'm not the Ghost of Christmas Present," Larry snorted.

"You're not part of my present at all. You decided to stay in Marbleheart with Mrs. Horsehair."

"Mrs. Horsehair is a kind mistress to serve. And I had no choice. You sold me!"

Cornell blinked in surprise. How rude of Mrs. Horsehair to share that secret with Larry!

"What's a poor benevolent supernatural sleuth to do? If I charged a fair rate, the people who needed me most couldn't afford me! I have to live, too, you know! Now just…"

Cornell pointed in the direction of Marbleheart. "Now just go back to Mrs. Horsehair where you belong and chew your cud there!"

"I can't do that, Professor. I am the Llama of Cornell Present, and I am here to help you with your attachment issues."

"I don't have attachment issues!"

"Oh, no? Then why didn't you go to prom?"

"You were there! I was perfecting a magic trick!"

"You were too afraid to spend an entire evening with the very pretty Amy Whitefield!"

"Who?"

"See? Attachment issues."

"This is stupid! I'm leaving!"

Cornell picked up his cord and

marched on bare feet down the grassy hill. If he kept walking, he might run into the hospital.

Or he might run into someone who, by the very sight of seeing a man in a hospital gown walking through the town, point out the way to the hospital.

And feel sorry enough for Cornell as to gift him with a bag of potato chips and a bottle of orange drink.

Larry's hooves thudded behind him.

"Professor," Larry gasped as he caught up with him. "I know you're lonely."

"I am not lonely. Ow!"

Cornell stopped to rub his big toe where he stubbed it on a sharp pebble.

"If you had a friend, a companion of sorts, you two could go out to dinner together."

"Why? I eat dinner just fine by myself in the motor home."

"You could go to the movies together."

"Why? I can listen to operas by myself in the motor home."

"Fine," Larry conceded. "Maybe you're not lonely. But you can treat people nicer."

Cornell stopped in his tracks, and

Larry stopped in his. Neither had reason to keep walking. The grassy hill was an everlasting hill, with no bottom to reach.

"What's wrong with the way I treat people? I solve their supernatural mysteries. I'm a gift to their world!"

"Yeah? These two ladies don't think so."

A very sick Cornell staggered across the room

"It's him!" the receptionist cried.

"I don't believe it," the nurse agreed. "After all this time."

"He has a lot of nerve!"

"Help me!" Cornell cried. "I'm very, very, very sick.

Calmly, the receptionist set aside her account book and picked up the chart.

Smiling, the nurse reached for the telephone and began to dial.

"Of course we'll help you," the receptionist said with a nod.

"McLouie's?" the nurse said. "I'd like one large pepperoni pizza."

The nurse covered the receiver and looked straight at Cornell. "Just as soon as we finish lunch."

"Why weren't they in a hurry to help you, Professor?"

Cornell held up his hands. "Larry, it was all a simple mistake. And stop chewing."

"I have to chew, or I'll be sick. Maybe you should eat less and chew more."

"Yuck!"

"Hey, I'm not the guy lying in a hospital bed. Now who are these two ladies, and what did you do to them?"

"I told you. It was a simple mistake. They hired me to do banish a poltergeist in the house they bought."

"Which you didn't do," Larry said, still chewing.

"Yes, I did!"

"Oh, you chanted some mumbo jumbo. And then you charged them a lot of money. So much that they couldn't afford to turn the house into the bed and breakfast they wanted! And for what? For what, Professor? For a loose shutter? The one you fixed with a cheap hammer and a couple of nails?"

Cornell turned away. Larry pranced over to face him.

"You didn't expect them to run into the original owner, did you?" The one who would say, 'Ah, I see you fixed the shutter. The banging used to keep me up all night!'"

"A carpenter would have charged them, too. And they got the spell as a bonus. No poltergeist would dare set foo..."

"Be quiet." Larry pricked up his ears. "Do you hear that?"

Cornell listened hard. "The ringing?"

Then Cornell noticed the phone booth.

"Answer the phone, Professor. I think the call is for me."

"Then answer your own phone call."

Larry held up a hoof. "Really?"

"Arggh!"

Frustrated, hungry, and thirsty, Cornell stomped to the phone booth and picked up the receiver. "Hello?"

"Hello, Professor," the woman's voice said at the other end. "Would you please send Larry home? I've got his dinner all ready."

"Fine," Cornell said and hung up. "You were right," he added as he emerged from the booth. "It was Mrs. Horsehair. She said to send..."

Cornell stopped.

Larry was gone.

In his place stood a photo booth.

Right in the middle of the grassy field stood a photo booth where no photo booth should be.

An unseen force pushed Cornell past the curtains and into the tunnel.

A voice from nowhere shouted, "Say cheese!"

Then a bright light blinded him.

CHAPTER TEN: PICTURE PERFECT

Cornell lay on a couch in the middle of a small living room. His eyes were closed, and his hand was touching his forehead.

Beyond him, in the attached dining room, also small, sat four rows of spectators. Their faces shone with anticipation.

Finally, Cornell sat up. His face looked sad.

"Friends," he said. "I am so sorry to disappoint you." He gestured to a tired-looking woman in the front row. "I'm especially sorry to disappoint you, Marilyn. I am unable to reach your uncle."

Marilyn burst into tears. "But he promised to take care of me! Why won't

Uncle Burke tell me where he hid the second will?"

Cornell rose, walked over to Marilyn, and gently patted her shoulder. "Perhaps he will another time. But since he was silent tonight, I shall not charge you."

Marilyn looked up at Cornell. Her face glowed with gratitude at his generosity.

"Oh, Professor, you are as kind as you are wise. Please stay for cake and coffee."

"I accept your gracious offer."

After allowing the other guests to take their place in the dessert line ahead of him, Cornell contented himself with the last crumbs of the cake and the remaining dribbles of cold coffee.

Then Cornell noticed her.

She was just an ordinary young woman, maybe even less than ordinary. She was a little chubby and parted her baby fine blonde hair to the side and held it in place with a gold barrette.

Her chinks were pink, and her blue eyes sparkled at the sight of him. But it was not the look on her face that startled Cornell.

It was the look on his.

Cornell saw a look on his face he'd never seen on anyone's face, certainly not the one he saw in the mirror each morning.

The future Cornell's eyes were bright, and his smile was soft and tender. With a start, Cornell realized he had seen that look earlier tonight.

It was the same look Charlie wore whenever he talked about Mabel.

"You did a wonderfully awesome job tonight!" the young woman said.

"You're too kind."

"It's not your fault Miss Bell's uncle didn't appear. I know with all my heart that if he will talk to someone, he will talk to you!"

"Thank you for your belief in me. I'm devastated I couldn't help." Cornell looked at her empty hands. "Didn't you get any cake?"

"Oh, I didn't need any sweets. The sweetest part of the night was talking to you!"

"Then let me buy you a cup of coffee, miss, er…"

"Katie, Katie Miller. And I'd be honored, Professor. I've never talked with a supernatural super sleuth."

The scene faded. Cornell was now standing in a dark room with no windows.

He had one companion: a man with oily hair parted down the middle, wearing round, silver, wire glasses and a white apron.

The man stood in front of a long counter. On the counter stood a row of white tubs filled liquid. An image lay in each tub.

One by one the man pulled out a wet image and hung it on the clothesline next to him. Then he picked up a deck of cards and handed them to Cornell.

"Are these yours?" the man asked.

Cornell took the cards. The first card was a picture of him lying on the couch. Cornell riffled the cards, and the entire séance he just experienced soundlessly repeated itself.

He looked up. The man continued hanging images. Cornell set the pack down on the counter, feeling he ought to speak since the other man did not.

"Oh, Cameraman of Christmas Future," Cornell said, pointing to the pack, "this should prove I'm fair, kind, not lonely, and don't have attachment issues. Now, if you'll just show me the way back to my hospital room, I'll…"

The cameraman picked up another deck of cards and handed it to Cornell.

Cornell was lying on the same couch in the middle of the same small living room. His eyes were closed, and his hand was touching his forehead.

Beyond him, in the attached dining room, also small, sat four rows of spectators. Their faces shone with anticipation.

"What else did Uncle Burke say? Is there a second will?"

"There is," Cornell intoned.

Marilyn clasped her hands and leaned forward, panting eagerly. "Ask him where he hid it?"

Cornell moaned. He wailed. He breathed hard. He breathed very quietly.

Finally, Cornell sat up. His face looked sad.

"Friends," he said. "I am so sorry to disappoint you." He gestured to a tired-looking woman in the front row. "I'm especially sorry to disappoint you, Marilyn.

Your uncle only said you would know where to find."

Marilyn burst into tears. "But he promised to take care of me! Why won't Uncle Burke tell me where he hid the second will?"

Cornell rose, walked over to Marilyn, and gently patted her shoulder. "Perhaps he will another time. Let me know if you don't find it. We can schedule a follow-up séance. In the meantime..."

He pulled a piece of paper from his pocket.

"...here is tonight's bill."

Marilyn looked at the bill and her face fell. "Professor, how do you expect me to pay..."

"And you promised cake," Cornell said. "Where is it? I hope the cake is as good as the cake in Cape Crag."

"It's in the dining room," Marilyn said, still anxious and scanning the bill.

Cornell strode to the dessert table, the guests respectfully allowing the great supernatural super sleuth to help himself first.

After taking two slices, he positioned

himself in the middle of the room, to best answer their questions and quote his prices.

Cornell again noted the chubby young woman with the baby fine blonde hair parted to the side and held in place with a gold barrette.

He noted the pink cheeks and the sparkling blue eyes. She was patiently waiting in line until he had spoken to the last guest.

But the future Cornell was too busy with his second slice of cake to notice.

"You did a wonderfully awesome job tonight!" the young woman said.

Cornell reached for the knife and cut himself another slice. As an afterthought, he cut a slice for the young woman and handed it to her.

She barely noticed, so entranced was she at his presence.

"I loved watching you in action tonight!" she exclaimed. "So authoritative with the spirits. So commanding of the situation. I just had to meet you! If you ever need help, I'd be happy to..."

"What is your name, miss, er..."

"Katie, Katie Miller."

"Well, I do have a sink filled with dishes that need washing. And I'm backed up in laundry, too."

Katie's eyes sparkled. "Oh, to enter the
enter the mysterious chambers of the great Professor Cornell Dyer! I'm so honored!"

Charlie spoke up. "You should be ashamed, Cornell. Is this any way to treat your future wife?"

"My what???"

Charlie waved his hand. "Look, Professor."

Cornell looked. He was standing with Charlie inside his motor home.

Two other people, teenagers, sat at his kitchen table. The boy had long red hair, a plain green T-shirt, and faded blue jeans. The girl, who had curly black hair much like Cornell's, wore a black T-shirt and jeans.

"Hey!" Cornell cried, waving his hands and pushing against a force field that held him in place.

Neither the boy nor the girl looked up. They were too busy handling one of Cornell's favorite crystal balls, which was not glowing as it should.

"Get out of my motor home!"

"They can't hear you," Charlie said. "These are visions from the future. You are not with them. They are not with you. But the girl: you don't recognize her?"

"Her hair looks like mine. And her eyes look like that Katie's...wait! You don't mean..."

"She's your daughter, Cornell."

"Then why am I not there guiding her, helping her?"

The girl gave the ball an impatient shake, and the ball glowed a sick green.

"No!" Cornell exploded. "Stop! You'll hurt it!"

Charlie shook his head and clucked his tongue.

"Why are you not there guiding her, Professor? I'll tell you why. Because you won't mend your ways. You're not lonely? Fine. But Katie is. Katie will miss you every day of the rest of her life. And Karla will have to struggle to carry on your legacy all by herself."

The scene darkened and vanished. Charlie vanished.

The world vanished, including everything real and everything most people wouldn't believe was real.

Cornell was absolutely, completely alone. He had nothing, and he had no one. He didn't even have darkness.

"Fine!" he cried out. "I'll do my own chores! I'll provide fair services. I'll be nicer to real and imaginary beings. Just don't leave me in this place of nothing!"

For the first time in his life, Cornell was alone. Along in the nothingness with nothing for company, not even an imaginary friend, not even a llama, much less a wife and a daughter.

Then he heard a voice cut through the void: "Cornell, can you hear me?"

EPILOGUE

"Yes," Cornell said as he opened his eyes.

He was lying in a propped-up hospital bed. A nurse with kind eyes was setting a tray full of covered dishes in front of him.

He did not see a gold cord, not from him nor from the nurse.

"Your temperature is normal," she said. "The doctor ordered a real breakfast for you. And by the way, 'Merry Christmas.'"

"Merry Christmas? So I haven't been here a long time?"

"Just overnight. Don't you remember?"

Cornell shook his head. "I had the strangest dreams."

"Well, your fever was pretty high. But that's behind you now." She felt his moist forehead with her cool hand. "The doctor will explain everything to you later."

"What's today's date?"

"Dec. 25. I told you. Today is Christmas Day."

The nurse was right. Not much time had passed at all.

She shut the door halfway on her way out. Cornell lifted one lid: watery poached eggs. He lifted a second: runny oatmeal.

He lifted a third: toast triangles lightly scraped with apricot jam. He lifted the fourth: quivering orange gelatin. He lifted the last: very, very weak, almost translucent tea.

No thick strips of crisp smoky bacon.

No sweet doughnuts liberally coated in powdered sugar, like Cape Crag, Maine after a heavy snowfall.

No potato chips. No orange drink.

Not even a candy cane or a chocolate Santa.

What kind of food was this?

But Cornell was hungry. So he ate it anyway. If he lost his strength, he could not solve supernatural mysteries and pay for the new spell book he HAD to have, the one sold online in 2020.

He was swallowing the last bite of dry toast when someone knocked on his door.

"Professor?"

A doctor poked his head around the door. He was short and stooped, with heavy, thick-rimmed black glasses and artificially dark hair slicked to one side.

A pipe, a beautiful pipe of polished dark wood and gold trim peeked out from his white lab coat pocket.

"Yes?" Cornell asked.

"I'm the doctor," the man said as he walked into the room reviewing Cornell's chart. "How are you feeling today?"

"Not sick at all. May I go home?"

"I think we can arrange it. Your fever is gone, and your vitals are normal."

"What happened to me?"

"You had the flu," the doctor said. "A very bad, very rare kind of flu. In fact, I've never diagnosed it in a human until yesterday."

Cornell's memory instantly transported him back to his last night in the motor home, before he caught the flu.

The room was dark except for the green glow of the phone dial, and the luminous dream fairies flitting through the rooms.

One of those fairies was sneezing.

And coughing.

And the fairy never covered its face with its wing.

Not once.

It just sneezed fairy sneezes all over the room as it flitted around Cornell's head and spread its germs all over Cornell. Just wait until he caught up with the fairy. Just wait.

But for now, he had a supernatural mystery to solve. And he had some questions for the doctor.

"Does this type of flu cause strange dreams?"

"Very strange dreams," the doctor said. "The strangest dreams you'll ever dream."

The doctor smiled kindly at Cornell. His green eyes reminded Cornell of a cat, full of wisdom and cunning.

Cornell did not like this doctor, and he did not know why.

But he also seemed familiar, as if Cornell had met him before today. But, again, Cornell did not know why.

"Just ring the nurse if you need anything," the doctor said. "In the meantime, we'll get your discharge papers ready. Would you like a newspaper to read?"

"Yes, thank you," Cornell said.

An hour later and happily browsing the day's news, Cornell encountered an obituary that nearly made him gasp.

Charlie Charleston, 86, of Turtle Tree, Nebraska passed away peacefully Dec. 24 at his home and is now happily reunited with his wife Mabel, his high school sweetheart and the love of his life, who passed away three years ago.

He was born on his family's farm to

the late *Charles Lee Charleston* and *Corinne (Jonoff) Charleston.*

Charlie attended *Turtle Tree Grade School* and graduated from *Turtle Tree High School.*

A farmer his entire life, Charlie will be remembered as one of the nicest people anyone could ever meet. He never liked to see a person in need and would help in every way he could.

Charles is preceded in death by his parents, grandparents, all ten siblings and his in-laws.

Staying behind to cherish his memories are Charlie's 13 children, 59 grandchildren, and 24 great-grandchildren...

A shrill ring made Cornell bolt up in bed, startling even the dream fairies floating the through the motor home.

He groped for the receiver and squinted at his luminous alarm clock. Not again!

"Madam!" Cornell exploded into the phone. 'Do you understand what time it is?"

"Yes! But as I keep telling you, it's the

only time the voice talk! Please, come right away and make them go away!"

"And as I keep telling you, I never go to work without a good night's rest and a really good breakfast!"

"Professor, I beg you...!"

"I will be there tomorrow morning. Right after I finish breakfast."

SYMBOLISM

In the nineteenth century, a writer named Charles Dickens wrote a story about Ebenezer Scrooge, who is visited by three Christmas spirits to help him let go of his unkind ways and become a caring person.

But long before Dickens wrote *A Christmas Carol*, people told ghost stories at Christmas, a tradition that dates to the Middle Ages.

The character of Charlie Charleston is loosely based on a character in the 1998 movie *Patch Adams*.

Harry Houdini was a famous illusionist in the early twentieth century.

Part of the belief in astral project is that a silver cord keeps people attached to their physical bodies.

The doctor and the white cats in the laboratory appear in other books in the Bryony Series.

Denise M. Baran-Unland is the author of the BryonySeries supernatural/literary trilogy for young and new adults, the Adventures of Cornell Dyer chapter book series for grade school children and the Bertrand the Mouse series for young children.
She has six adult children, three adult stepchildren, fourteen total grandchildren, six godchildren, and four cats.
She is the co-founder of WriteOn Joliet and previously taught features writing for a homeschool coop, with the students' work published in the co-op magazine and The Herald-News in Joliet.
Denise blogs daily and is currently the features editor at The Herald-News. To read her feature stories, visit www.theherald-news.com. For more information about Denise's fiction and to follow her on social media, visit www.bryonyseries.com.

Sue Midlock lives in Illinois with her husband and has been writing for 10 years. She started writing when the book "Twilight" first came out and fell in love with the paranormal genre.

Since then, she has written and finished her Rosewood Trilogy and just recently her anniversary edition, "Forever," which is the first book re-written for adults.

Her most recent releases are "Southern Shorts," which is an anthology of short stories about Dry Prong, Louisana and "Night Games."

Timothy Baran has enjoys cooking on professional and home levels. He also likes writing dark poetry and stories whose style mimics C. S. Lewis, his favorite author.

He is currently working on his first novel and a book of poetry.

But he especially loves his cat Midnight, whom he raised from a kitten.